The Alden Family Mysteries
by Gertrude Chandler Warner

THE BOXCAR CHILDREN
SURPRISE ISLAND
THE YELLOW HOUSE MYSTERY
MYSTERY RANCH
MIKE'S MYSTERY
BLUE BAY MYSTERY
THE WOODSHED MYSTERY
THE LIGHTHOUSE MYSTERY
MOUNTAIN TOP MYSTERY
SCHOOLHOUSE MYSTERY
CABOOSE MYSTERY
HOUSEBOAT MYSTERY
SNOWBOUND MYSTERY
TREE HOUSE MYSTERY
BICYCLE MYSTERY
MYSTERY IN THE SAND
MYSTERY BEHIND THE WALL
BUS STATION MYSTERY
BENNY UNCOVERS A MYSTERY

BUS STATION MYSTERY

GERTRUDE CHANDLER WARNER

Illustrated by David Cunningham

ALBERT WHITMAN & Company, Chicago

ISBN 0-8075-0976-0

5 7 9 10 8 6 4

Printed in the U.S.A.

Contents

CHAPTER		PAGE
1	"Wait Outside!"	9
2	Trouble Inside	20
3	No Bus in Sight	32
4	A Discovery	42
5	Not Fair!	53
6	What Did Happen?	68
7	The Snooper	79
8	Tricked Twice	87
9	Frank's Problem	97
10	Benny Guesses	105
11	Back to the Station	117

BUS STATION MYSTERY

CHAPTER 1

"Wait Outside!"

Listen—listen to this!" said Benny Alden. He was reading the newspaper after breakfast. "Science and Hobby Fair. Oakdale, July 25–26. The last day's today!"

"A two-day science and hobby fair?" asked Jessie. "That sounds interesting. I'd like to go."

Benny looked at Violet and Henry.

"Well, come on then," said Henry. "Let's all go! I'd like to see what other kids have invented and built all by themselves. Let me see the paper, Ben."

Then Henry read aloud, "One hundred exhibits by young people and adults. Special exhibits by factories to show what they make and show that Oakdale is a fast-growing town."

"How can we get there?" asked Jessie.

"We can ride our bikes to Oakdale," said Violet.

"Oh, no, Violet," Henry said. "Oakdale is thirty miles away. That's too far to bike both ways in one day."

"Well, what about the bus?" Benny asked. "We'll have to look at a bus timetable. But we haven't got a timetable."

"It just happens that I have a timetable," said Grandfather Alden. He took a timetable out of his pocket. "It's a brand new one," he said, "so it will be right." He gave the timetable to Henry.

Henry looked it over. "No," he said, "we can't go straight to Oakdale. We have to change buses at Plainville Junction, and we have to wait there an hour for the bus to Oakdale."

"That's OK," said Benny. "People always have to wait at stations for buses and trains. That's what stations are for."

Jessie said, "If we hurry, we can get the morning bus."

Grandfather Alden laughed. "Well, Benny, you've started something as usual. I wish I could come along, too. I know that there's a lot of new business around Oakdale. I hear something about a new company near Plainville Junction."

"What about lunch?" Benny asked.

They all laughed. Benny was always hungry, and he could always eat even when he was not hungry at all.

"I think there will be plenty to eat at the fair," Henry said. "Perhaps at the bus station, too."

"Yes, I think so," said Mr. Alden. "As I remember it, the bus station is at a crossroads in a lonely spot. The station is near a red bridge over the river. Not many people live around there."

"We can wait till we get to the fair in Oakdale," Jessie decided. "I'm sure we can eat there."

"Look up a bus that will bring us home, Henry,"

Benny said. "If there are buses at the right time, we can go and come back all in one day."

Henry looked at the timetable again and found a return bus that would bring them back by dinnertime. He looked around at the others and said, "This is one time we don't have to pack a bag or a lunch or take a thing."

"Better take a little money," said Grandfather with a smile.

"For bus tickets," agreed Henry.

"And for something to eat," put in Benny.

"Perhaps we'd better take raincoats," Jessie added. "We've been caught in plenty of showers."

"It won't rain," objected Benny. "Look at that blue sky!"

Mr. Alden shook his head. "I'd call this day a weather breeder. Better take your raincoats. This is just the time of year for a sudden storm."

So with money and four raincoats, the Aldens started off for the Oakdale Hobby Fair. They got to the Greenfield bus station just in time to catch the bus for Plainville Junction.

"You can get tickets to Oakdale at the Plainville

bus station," the driver told them. "I suppose you are going to the fair."

"That's right," answered Benny.

There was only one other person on the bus, an old gentleman. Jessie and Violet sat together, and Henry took a seat behind the bus driver. Ben sat down with the old gentleman. He liked company, and he liked to meet strangers.

"Just going somewhere for the day?" asked the old man with a smile.

"Yes, we're going to Oakdale to the hobby fair," Benny answered. "Are you going to Oakdale, too?"

"No, I'm not going to change at the junction. I'm going right through. I have a long trip before me. I'm going to Ohio."

"If you come from Ohio," Benny said, "you don't know this part of the country very well."

"Well, yes, I do. I grew up in New England near Plainville Junction. But I moved out to Ohio about ten years ago. I come here once in a while to visit my old friends in Greenfield and in Oakdale."

Benny said, "You must have had a good time visiting everyone."

The old gentleman smiled. "Yes, I did. But every-thing is changing. Some of it's good and some of it's bad. Or that's what people told me."

Benny and the man talked about the things they passed, and the time went by quickly. In a little while the bus came to flat countryside.

"My grandfather says no one lives around here," remarked Benny as they rode along. "Everything is deserted."

The man laughed. "You mean *was* deserted. You'll see what I mean when you get out at the bus station. I had to change buses there to get to Greenfield. The man in the station is all stirred up about what's going on. He says there's going to be a big fight."

"A fight?" asked Benny. "About what?"

"Some kind of factory. Some people think it's good because there is more work. Other people are afraid the river will be spoiled. Polluted, you know."

"Yes, I know about pollution," replied Benny. He looked out the bus window. He saw that the road was running along beside a little river. Up ahead he could see a red bridge.

"The station is right around the next bend," the

old man said. "Three highways come together. That's why it's called Plainville Junction. The bus for Oakdale will cross the bridge and pick you up. It's about ten miles to Oakdale."

Just then the bus came to a stop. They were at Plainville Junction.

Benny picked up his raincoat and said good-bye to the old gentleman.

"The man who runs the station is named Frank," the old man called after him. "Ask him how he likes his new neighbors."

The old man laughed, and Benny guessed it was some kind of joke. But maybe not a funny joke.

The Aldens looked around. Mr. Alden was right. The bus station seemed to be all by itself except for some big trees. There was not a house to be seen. There was not even any traffic on any of the three roads that met at the junction.

A sign said "Frank's Place," and under it, "Bus Station."

The four Aldens climbed down from the big air-conditioned bus. It was already a hot day. Benny sniffed. "What an awful smell," he said.

But Benny did not have more time to think about the air. Suddenly the door of the bus station flew open. Two boys—older than Benny but younger than Henry—came flying down the steps. Right behind the boys came a man with a cook's apron on.

"Don't come around here again!" he shouted. "I don't need help from any of your family. Just mind your own business. If you want to take a bus, you can wait outside."

The boys jumped down the rest of the steps. The man in the apron slammed the door shut.

"Well, well," said Henry softly. "Our trip isn't beginning very well. I wonder what those boys did to make that man so mad."

Violet added, "I wonder if that cook was Frank."

The two boys glanced at the Aldens and at the bus. Then they ran over to a big tree and threw themselves on the grass in the shade.

Benny looked up at the friendly old man in the bus window and waved. The man smiled and waved back. There were no more new passengers. The bus driver honked his horn to show that he was leaving. Then the big bus pulled away.

The Aldens stood together, looking from the bus station to the two boys.

"What do we do now?" asked Jessie.

"We go in and buy our tickets," Henry said calmly. "That quarrel has nothing to do with us."

"But what about that cross man in the bus station?" asked Violet. "I don't like to have people shouting at us."

"He isn't going to shout at *us*," Henry said with a laugh. "We haven't done anything to annoy him. Those boys must have done something he didn't like."

"Must have been something big," Benny said. "Was he ever mad!"

While the Aldens were talking, the mailman came along in his car. "Are you going into the station?" he asked the Aldens. "Hand this letter to Frank, will you?"

Benny said, "Sure," and took the letter. It was a thick letter with the name Frank Timmons typed on the front. It looked like a business letter. Benny couldn't help seeing the printing in the corner of the envelope. A large, bright-colored paint can was printed in the corner. Paint running out spelled the slogan, "Pickett's Perfect Paints."

"Come on," Henry called. "Let's see if the bus for Oakdale is on time."

He went up the steps to the station and opened the door. Benny was the last one to enter. He thought he heard the two boys under the tree laugh as he went in.

Were they laughing at him? Benny didn't know.

CHAPTER 2

Trouble Inside

The bus station really turned out to be a small lunchroom. There was a counter on one side, and along one wall were some small tables with chairs pushed up to them. There was one bigger table. Near the door was a bench where passengers could wait for the bus.

The man who had just slammed the door looked up as the door opened. He held a watering can, and he was watering a plant at one end of the room.

"You're Frank, aren't you?" said Henry at once.

"Yes, I'm Frank," the man said shortly. "What do you want? It's too early for lunch. I haven't made any sandwiches yet." He didn't smile.

The four Aldens were thinking the same thing. This man was not very polite. In fact, he was not a good man to run a lunch counter in a bus station.

"Do you sell bus tickets?" asked Benny as if nothing had happened.

"Yes," answered Frank, "and I run this lunch counter."

Benny explained, "We are going to Oakdale to the hobby fair. We have to change buses here to get to Oakdale. Is that right?"

"That's right," said Frank, not so crossly. "But the bus to Oakdale will be late today. You may have to wait here an hour."

"Yes," said Jessie, nodding. "We expected to wait here an hour, even before we started from Greenfield. We don't mind."

"This is a nice station to wait in," added Violet. She was thinking about the two boys Frank had told to wait outside.

Benny went over to the counter and said, "If you are Frank, I think this is your letter."

Without saying thank you Frank took the letter and threw it on a shelf behind the counter. But he said to the Aldens, "You can wait here. Do anything you like. Sit down. Walk around. It's pretty hot outside."

His voice was pleasant now as he spoke to the Aldens. It was plain that he liked them better than the two young boys.

The Aldens folded their raincoats across the wooden bench. They all sat down.

Henry asked, "Can we buy our tickets now from you?"

"Yes, indeed," said Frank.

"We want just one-way tickets," Henry said quickly. "The bus driver told us we could buy our return tickets at Oakdale."

"Right," said Frank, handing four tickets to Henry.

Violet was looking out of a window. "Oh, dear," she said, "I hope it doesn't start to rain. Just the same, we're lucky that we brought our raincoats."

The others looked out. Dark clouds were beginning to fill the western sky. But the leaves on the trees hardly stirred.

"No need to worry about the rain," said Frank. "This won't last long. You can keep dry if you wait inside."

Benny suddenly remembered the bad smell outdoors. Now he said, "Oh, we'll wait inside for sure. The air outside smells just terrible."

Frank's face changed. He looked angry. "That's my new neighbor," he said gruffly. "New neighbors —they have no business here. I don't have any use for neighbors of that kind."

The Aldens were puzzled. But they did not dare ask any questions. Did the man mean the two boys or did he mean someone else?

Frank turned his back to the Aldens. They sat still on the bench and watched him.

The telephone rang. In the quiet room it sounded loud. Violet jumped.

Frank went over to the wall telephone and picked up the receiver. "Frank speaking," he said.

Someone began to talk and Frank started to frown. "Yes, I just got your letter," he said. "No, I haven't opened it. I told you I wasn't interested. You can't offer me enough."

Frank started to hang up, but the voice on the line didn't give up.

"What?" Frank asked. "You'll do what? Is that what you wrote in your letter? Well, I'd like to see you try. That's all, I'd just like to see you try. You can't do something like that to me. I'll find a way to stop you."

Frank put the receiver back in place without saying good-bye. He frowned angrily. Then his face changed. He had the saddest look that the Aldens had almost ever seen.

The Aldens looked at each other. Something was certainly going on. Here was a man who could be angry one minute and sad the next. Why was he so troubled?

Benny muttered in Henry's ear, "A deep and dark secret."

Frank reached up and turned on a radio. Jessie thought that Frank felt the music would be better than his silence.

No one said anything for a little while. Frank washed some cups at the sink behind the lunch counter.

Suddenly the music stopped in the middle of a song. A radio announcer's voice broke in. "This is a National Weather Service warning. A tornado watch is in effect in York and Plain counties. High winds expected, with some thunderstorms. We will give you more information when we have it. Stay tuned to this station for up-to-date storm bulletins."

Violet was pale. All the Aldens looked out at the day that now looked so dark and stormy.

Frank looked at Violet kindly and said, "A tornado watch only means we might have a bad storm. Now, if it were a tornado *warning* then it would be much worse." He was trying to make Violet feel better.

Henry and Frank walked to the door and stepped outside. They saw that the wind had begun to blow the dust on the road in front of the station. The tree branches swayed in the strong wind.

Henry looked for the two boys under the tree, but they had gone.

Violet peeked outside. "Look at those black clouds, Jessie. They're moving so fast!"

The sun had gone behind the clouds. The sky was growing darker by the minute.

Frank and Henry came back inside and shut the door. Frank turned to the Aldens. They could see he was worried.

"I have a little house on the river just a mile from here," Frank said. "I think I left the windows open this morning. Maybe I should go back and close up the house before the storm hits. I have a small boat pulled up on the riverbank. I want to see that it is tied tightly to its post so that it won't float off in the storm."

"It's all right with us if you go," Benny said. "But is it safe for you outside?"

"Oh, don't worry about me," Frank said. "I'll be safe. I have a car parked behind the building here. I can drive over to my house in just a few minutes. I can get there before the rain starts. If I get caught, I'll stay in my house until it is over."

"You'll come back here, won't you?" asked Violet.

"Oh, yes, I'll come right back to the bus station. You'll be all right if you stay in the station. This is a strong brick building. It doesn't leak."

"We'll be fine," Jessie said. "We won't go outside unless the bus comes to take us to Oakdale."

"Yes," said Frank. "If the bus comes, you can just shut the station door as you leave. The door will lock if you shut it tight. When I come back, I can open the door with my key. I don't expect anyone to stop at the station anyway. Everyone will see the storm coming and stay indoors. Too bad for the hobby fair. There won't be a crowd on a day like this."

"We'll keep the radio on and listen for the weather bulletins," Henry said. "I'm sure everything will be all right. Don't worry about us."

Frank walked to the door to go out. Then he stopped as if he had remembered something. He turned to the Aldens and really smiled. "You four might get hungry while I'm gone. You can just look in the refrigerator and take whatever you'd like."

"Why, thank you," said Jessie. She was surprised. "That's very good of you."

Benny added, "We'll look in the refrigerator the minute you're gone. Be sure of that."

Frank laughed. "You can just leave the money by the cash register," he said. "I'll know what it is for."

He smiled again and waved good-bye. Then he walked out and shut the door behind him.

But a moment later the door opened. There stood Frank. This time he looked angry again.

"I forgot to tell you something," he said. "If you see two boys hanging around, don't let them in. They are troublemakers. I don't want to have anything to do with them."

Then Frank turned around and went out. This time he passed the window, and in a minute or so the Aldens heard him start his car. He drove off down the road that ran close to the river.

"Well," said Benny. "What do you make of that? First Frank is friendly and thinks we might get hungry. And then he gets angry and tells us to watch out for those boys he doesn't like. I don't understand what makes him act so."

Jessie said thoughtfully, "Frank knows those boys and we don't. Nobody would order them out of a public bus station unless they had done something very annoying."

Benny said, "Well, so far it's a mystery to us. We don't understand anything about it. But I know one thing. I'm not going to ask Frank about it and get my head taken off."

Jessie glanced quickly around the bus station. She began to see a lot of interesting things.

"Look at those beautiful pink flowers on the windowsill," she said. "They're on all the windowsills. Frank must love flowers."

"Birds, too," added Benny, looking out of the window. "Just look at the bird houses. And there are some bird feeding stations, too."

Violet said, "A man who likes birds and flowers can't be all bad. Just look at that woodpecker! Isn't his red head beautiful! Oh, it's flying away. Something must have scared it."

Henry was looking over Violet's shoulder. He saw the bird, too. But he saw something else as well. He was sure that something moved behind one of the trees.

Henry continued to watch. He caught sight of a red shirt. It must be one of the two boys Frank had sent out of the bus station in such a hurry.

Henry had been wondering what had become of the boys. Had one of them been spying on the Aldens? Or maybe the boys were watching Frank. That was possible, too.

Henry didn't want to say anything to frighten Violet or Jessie. But Benny exclaimed, "Hey, I see somebody behind the station. Who is it? One of those kids! Sneaking around, that's what. No wonder Frank is mad."

"Wait a minute," Jessie said. "I don't think the boy is sneaking around. He has field glasses. He was watching the bird Violet saw."

For a few minutes it seemed as if the storm was not going to be too bad. Perhaps the tornado watch was already over.

Then all at once the sky turned a deep purple. The wind which had died down suddenly returned with new strength. The bus station sign creaked and tree branches bent in the strong gusts. The Aldens backed away from the windows.

CHAPTER 3

No Bus in Sight

Frank hadn't been gone more than a few minutes, and now the wind was howling.

The four Aldens walked to the front windows of the bus station-lunchroom. The sky was darker than ever, and the dust was whirling around in the air.

"Here comes the rain," Benny exclaimed. And sure enough, the raindrops began to fall. The big drops fell slowly at first, and Violet watched them hit the windowpanes. Then the drops began to fall faster and harder. Rain pounded on the windows.

"I wonder where those kids are," said Henry.

Violet replied, "Well, wherever they are, they are soaking wet. I know Frank said not to let them in, but just the same, I think we ought to."

Benny laughed. "We don't know their names. What should we call? 'Boys? Hey, boys!' 'Hello, you boys!' Or, 'Come here, you kids!' "

Just then there was a knocking at the door. It sounded very loud, even over the howling wind.

Benny said, "I don't care! You can't just leave somebody outside in a storm like this. You can't!"

Henry went to the door and unbolted it. The wind tore it out of his hand and two very wet boys stumbled in.

The door banged and Henry struggled to pull it shut. Now he was nearly as wet as the boys who'd just come in.

Water dripped in a puddle around each boy. Their hair hung down over their eyes. Water ran from the backpacks they were wearing.

"Thanks very much," said one of the boys. "It's a trifle damp outside."

"So we see," Henry replied. "That's why we let you in. You know we weren't supposed to let you in. Frank didn't want anyone to come in."

"Yes, we know," the boy in the blue shirt said. "But Frank is sure all mixed up about us."

The boy in the red shirt said, "Don't worry about us. We'll get right out as soon as the storm is over. It won't last long."

Jessie said, "I wonder if Frank got to his house before the rain started."

"Sure," said the older boy. "He had lots of time. Anyway, his house is just as safe as the bus station."

Benny thought to himself how queer it was that the boy didn't sound angry at Frank. He sounded almost worried about him.

These boys were not strangers at Plainville Junction. They knew too much about Frank. They were not the new neighbors the old man on the bus had mentioned. The Aldens would just have to keep their ears open. Somehow they were sure they'd find out who Frank's new neighbors were.

By now Benny was really curious about the boys. They seemed restless and did not sit down. The Aldens watched the older boy wander all around the bus station, even behind the counter where the refrigerator was. He seemed to glance at an envelope.

"Hey, Troy," he said, talking to his brother. "Guess what? Frank got a letter from Pickett's Perfect Paints. He hasn't even opened it."

"Why should he, Jud?" returned Troy. "Frank probably knows what is in it."

The boys were right, Benny thought suddenly. Frank had had that telephone call. That was how he had learned what the letter was about. Now Benny was sure the call must have been from someone at the paint factory.

Rain beat against the window and Violet said, "Look at it pour. It hasn't rained so hard in weeks. Now I know what Grandfather meant about today being a weather breeder. Bad weather."

Off in the distance the Aldens could hear the thunder roar. The lightning made the sky bright for a moment. Then came the thunder. Benny looked at Jessie just as one bright flash came.

The thunder rumbled again.

"It can't rain this hard very long," Henry said. "I think the storm will be over soon."

One of the boys stared out of the windows. "No funnel cloud," he said. "It's a bad storm, but it's no tornado."

Just as he spoke, lightning lit up the sky and the bus station. A great clap of thunder sounded, followed by a crash.

"That was close!" Benny said. "Too close!"

"Something got hit, that's sure," the boy in the red shirt said.

"We're safe," Benny said. "Or as safe as anyone can be in a thunder shower."

"But that crash was awfully close," Jessie said in a worried voice. "I hope lightning didn't strike a tree nearby."

Henry said, "Who would have thought this day would have changed so quickly? First a beautiful blue sky without a cloud, then suddenly a black sky with nothing but clouds?"

Jessie said, "We're dry anyway. Come on, Violet. Let's sit on this bench away from the windows."

"Yes," agreed Henry. "You do that."

But one of the boys peered out into the storm. Then he whistled. "Hey, it was a tree that got hit. The very tree we were lying under. Wow! Are we lucky we're safe inside. Thanks again for letting us in."

"You're welcome," said Benny politely. "You have just as much right to be here as we do."

The storm seemed to leave as quickly as it had come. The lightning was not as bright, the thunder not as loud. The wind stopped lashing the trees.

In a short time, the sky became brighter.

Henry went to the window and announced, "The worst of the storm is over now. It's hardly raining at all. In a few minutes we can go outside and see what happened."

The two strange boys, Troy and Jud, shook themselves and pushed their hair back. They picked up their backpacks.

"We don't want to be here when Frank comes back," the big boy said. "No sense in making him mad all over again. He's going to be upset enough about losing that big oak tree. It was a beauty."

"Yeah," the other boy said. "It isn't fair. Frank loves trees. He knows all the trees and birds and plants around here."

"Not like some people who don't care at all," the boy in the red shirt said.

Henry opened the door slowly, and they all went out. Branches and twigs were scattered about, blown down by the wind.

"The rain's stopped now," Benny said. "Say, how good everything smells. Not the way it did when we got off the bus."

The boys laughed, and one said, "We know all about that."

The Aldens walked around to the side of the bus station. They had to step over the deep puddles.

Jessie was the first one to get a good look at what had happened. "Oh, yes! You were right," she said, looking at the big boy. "Lightning did strike that tree. And it's taken some wires down with it!"

"Stand back," Henry said. "Don't go near any fallen wires."

The big boy said, "Those are telephone wires, not wires for electricity."

"Sure," said Benny. "The lights didn't go off in the bus station."

"No telephone!" said Violet. "We can't make any calls. And no one can call us."

"Well," Benny said cheerfully, "nobody but Frank knows we're here."

The four Aldens and the two boys walked all around the station. The smaller boy picked up one of the bird feeders and put it carefully back in the tree.

"What time is it, Henry?" Jessie asked.

Henry looked at his watch. "It's half past twelve. That Oakdale bus is really late."

Benny said, "Frank told us that the bus would be late. He said we'd have to wait an hour. But it's more than that now."

Benny and Henry looked out toward the road in front of the station. They looked to the right and left. They could not see any traffic. No cars, no trucks, no bus.

"What do you think of that, Henry?" Benny asked. "Not a car in sight."

"Maybe people are waiting to make sure the storm

is over," Henry suggested. "That would be smart." But he thought to himself that something was wrong.

The two boys said, "We've got something to do. You kids stay at the station. See you later." And they disappeared down the road.

"I thought they wanted the Oakdale bus, too," Benny said slowly. "Do you think they changed their minds?"

"I don't know," Henry said, shrugging. "There's a lot we don't know about this bus trip."

The Aldens went back into the station building to wait for the bus.

CHAPTER 4

A Discovery

The minutes went by, but no bus pulled up in front of the station. Frank did not come back either. The strange boys were gone, but nobody knew where. Not even a car passed.

Benny finally spoke up. "It's one o'clock now. That's long past lunchtime, and I'm hungry. Why don't we have some lunch? Frank told us we could. So it will be OK with him."

"Yes, why not?" Jessie said. "There's no telling when the bus will come. I'm hungry, too."

"So am I," Henry said.

That settled it. Jessie and Violet went behind the lunch counter and opened the refrigerator and looked in. They found butter, milk, and hamburgers. In the breadbox were hamburger rolls and loaves of bread for sandwiches.

"That's enough," Jessie said with a nod. "These are just the things Frank uses for his lunch counter. We can get up a good meal."

"Just hurry," Benny said.

Jessie got out a frying pan and began to cook the hamburgers. Soon the smell was delicious. Everyone began to sniff.

"Come right up to the counter, ladies and gentlemen," said Jessie. "Here are paper plates and paper cups." She poured four cups of milk.

"Isn't there anything else in the refrigerator, Jessie?" Benny asked.

"Well, Ben!" exclaimed Henry. "Right in front of your eyes. Look at that glass doughnut jar on the counter."

"Well, well," said Benny. "I guess I'm blind or something. Doughnuts and milk will finish this lunch off just fine."

"Wait, Benny. Let me look again," said Jessie. "There was another package in the refrigerator." She opened the door and took out the package.

"Cheese!" shouted Benny. "I know it's cheese before you get the paper off. I hope it's the kind I like."

It was cheese and the kind Benny liked. More milk and lunch was over.

"Not many dishes to wash," said Jessie, laughing. She threw away the paper cups and plates. "No spoons, and not even knives and forks. I'll just wash the frying pan," she said as she scrubbed away. She left it clean and shiny and she hung it up under the counter.

Henry looked at his watch again. "I wonder where Frank is. He should have come back by now."

"No sign of the bus, either," said Benny. "We'll never get to the fair in Oakdale at this rate. Not much of an adventure, just waiting in a bus station."

Just then there were voices outside. "You still here?" someone called. It wasn't Frank.

Benny ran to look out. The two strange boys were back. They had on dry clothes. They both grinned at the Aldens.

The big boy said, "We just went home to dry out. We found out we wouldn't miss the bus. We could take our time."

"How did you find out?" Henry asked.

The smaller boy said, "Because the wind blew a big dead tree across the road that leads to the bridge. Nobody can get through. The bus has to go miles around the other way."

"The highway is closed!" said Violet in a low voice. "That means we're stranded. Grandfather will be worried about us. I wish we could call him in Greenfield. But the telephone line is broken."

"Don't worry about Grandfather," Henry said. "He won't know we are stuck at this little bus station. I'm sure he thinks we are in Oakdale now, enjoying the fair."

"Come on," the older boy said. "Let's go back down to the road and watch for the highway patrol to come. See you kids later." And the two boys ran off.

"I don't like this very much," said Benny. "Nothing to do. I wish I had something to look at."

Jessie said, "Well, when I was cleaning up I did see something that made me curious."

"You did?" Benny asked. "Anything will be better than nothing."

Jessie said, "I didn't say anything about it, because I didn't think it was any of our business. Still, it is different from what you'd expect in a bus station."

"What are you talking about?" asked Henry. He was curious now, too.

Jessie said, "Come around behind the counter. Look up on that high shelf."

They all looked up. There were several drinking glasses half full of dirty water. Two glasses held old faded weeds, and one glass held clean water and bright green weeds. There were many test tubes in a wire rack, each labeled with the name of a chemical. Beside the glasses were several books and a few notebooks.

"I can see the name of one of those books from down here," said Violet. "It is *How to Analyze Water*."

"One of them is a bird book," said Jessie in astonishment. "Imagine a bird book in a bus station!"

Violet said, "That bird book is exactly like the one Grandfather has. It has colored pictures of every bird in this part of the country."

"Now why didn't I see all this before?" demanded Benny.

"Well, Ben," replied Henry, laughing, "you don't go looking around near the ceiling when it's pouring and blowing like a tornado and two boys are hiding and acting mysterious. But we've seen all these test tubes and books now, and it means that Frank is all the more of a riddle. He must be a strange man."

Benny took a chair and put it under the shelf. He climbed up on it.

"Don't touch anything, Benny," said Jessie.

"Oh, no," answered Benny. "In the first place, these things belong to Frank. In the second place, I don't want to leave any fingerprints."

Then Benny exclaimed, "Oh, *now* I can see what I'm doing! Now guess what! Here is another big book on the other side of the glasses. It's called *Chemistry of Paints and Varnishes*. Is Frank a chemist *and* a bus station man *and* a lunchroom keeper *and* a gardener?"

"Maybe Frank is doing some work for the paint factory," Jessie suggested.

"Maybe chemistry is just his hobby," said Violet. "He hasn't very much to work with. Only a few bottles and a book."

"Frank has so many hobbies," said Benny. "Remember the bird feeders and the bird houses and the flowers in the windows. I wish he would come back so we could talk with him."

"I think those boys, Jud and Troy, were bothering Frank while he was working," said Jessie. "He certainly wanted to get rid of them."

"Maybe he thought they were watching him. Remember the field glasses," Benny said.

Henry started to say something. But he heard the noise of a car turning around in front of the bus station.

"That must be Frank," Violet said quickly.

It was Frank. "Everything OK?" he called. "No bus yet?"

"We're fine," said Jessie, "but no bus. Did you

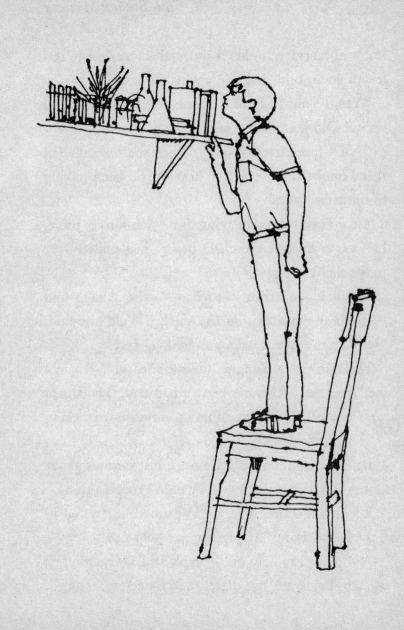

know the bridge is closed by a fallen tree? The bus has to go around, and that's why it's late."

"Yes, I know," replied Frank. "But how did *you* know? Did you walk down to the bridge?"

"No," Jessie started to say. Then she remembered that Frank wouldn't like to hear they'd been talking to those two boys.

But Frank was not paying any attention to Jessie. He was staring at the chair Benny had pulled over to the shelf.

Frank looked from the chair to the Aldens and then up at the books on the shelf. "Well," he said, "what in the world were you looking for?"

He didn't sound angry. He sounded sad. "Excuse me," he said. "This has been a bad day. The storm . . . one of my big trees blown down by lightning . . . the kids pestering me . . ."

Benny said quickly, "We were just curious about all those weeds and things. We didn't touch a thing."

Violet added in a hurry. "We are all interested in flowers and plants. Maybe we can help you."

"Nobody can help me," Frank said. "The thing is too big. I've tried, but there is too much against me."

He seemed to be speaking to himself, not to the Aldens. He seemed to have forgotten they were there.

Then there was a loud honk outside.

"The bus for Oakdale!" Benny cried. "Oh, we mustn't miss it! We've waited so long."

Frank shook his head as if to get rid of his troubles. "You won't miss it," he told Benny. "The driver will wait."

Henry took out the tickets, and the four Aldens filed out of the bus station. Frank followed.

The bus driver was standing beside the bus, unlocking the baggage compartment. He looked around and waved at Frank. "More passengers?" he asked.

Frank nodded. "They have their tickets."

The driver lifted the door of the baggage compartment as he said, "I've got a package for Pickett, Plainview Junction. Not very big—now where is it? Oh, here it is."

"That's all?" Frank said. "Nothing else?"

"That's it," the driver said. He looked at the Aldens. "You can give me your tickets now. All aboard!"

The Aldens went up the steps to the bus. It was dark inside.

Benny looked around. If Jud and Troy had already climbed in, he could not see them.

The driver slammed the big door shut. "Oakdale in fifteen minutes," he announced.

The Aldens settled back in their seats, glad to be on their way to the fair at last.

CHAPTER 5

Not Fair!

Benny and Henry sat together on the bus. They rode along without saying anything for a few minutes. Then Benny said, "I'd like to know what Frank was talking about. It's just as if we stepped into the middle of a mystery."

Henry smiled. "We're always doing that, Ben. But if we could just find out what is wrong, we might help."

"Do you think it's those two boys?" Benny asked. Then he answered his own question. "I don't."

"We know Frank is interested in birds and gardens and weeds," Henry said. "The chemicals and books make me think he knows a lot about chemistry. I suppose he could be doing some work for the paint company. He took a package from the driver."

Benny thought a minute. "That man on the morning bus told me to ask Frank about his new neighbors. I wonder why." He couldn't think of any reason.

Henry and Benny stopped talking. Everyone on the bus was quiet except for a man who was snoring and a crying baby.

Then someone began to talk. Benny found himself listening. He heard a boy's voice. "Wait till he gets a good start. Be ready when I give the signal."

"Yeah," another voice answered. "I'll be ready. I'm not scared, and I don't care what he says."

The first voice sounded angry. "You don't understand. We don't care about *him*. We know he'll be mad at us. It's the people who are there who are important. Don't forget that."

The boys stopped talking. Benny didn't dare look around to see who had been speaking. But he was sure he knew. They were the two boys Frank had sent out of the bus station, the two boys who had laughed at the Aldens. What could they be planning?

The younger boy started to talk again. "OK. I understand. What about the meeting tomorrow night? Do you think we can get in?"

"We can try," the older boy said. "Frank will be there. I'm sure of that."

"Shhh," the younger boy whispered. "Somebody may be listening."

"You mean those girls behind us? They don't know what we're talking about."

"You can't tell," the other boy said. "I don't trust anybody."

Benny wanted to look around at Jessie and Violet. Were they sitting behind the whispering boys? It was hard to think anyone wouldn't trust them!

"Oakdale!" the bus driver called. "Ten-minute rest stop." He swung the handle that opened the big bus door.

Benny and Henry were the first ones to get off the bus. Violet and Jessie followed them.

Benny didn't want the two boys from Plainville Junction to think he was watching for them. He saw a hobby fair poster. "Look," he called. "Here's an advertisement. Let's ask someone how to get there."

When he looked around a minute later, Benny saw the boys with their backpacks hurrying away from the bus. By the time the Aldens had been told the directions, the boys were out of sight.

The hobby fair was in the town hall. Tables had been set up for the displays. Some people met the Aldens as they were buying their tickets. A stranger smiled at Benny and said, "You're going to be surprised when you see this fair."

"Why?" asked Benny.

"Well, there are a lot of things you'd never think of. You must go and see the clock with three round faces. It tells the time and the month and the temperature. The three faces go round and round. You can stand and watch it for a long time."

"Thank you," said Henry. "We'll go right to the clock."

But when they reached the clock, the crowd was huge. The Aldens could not get near it.

"We'll never see it," Jessie said.

"Never mind," said Benny. "We can come back to see the clock later. I just saw a sign that says 'Fishermen's Corner.' We've just got to see that."

A crowd of men and boys were looking at a board covered with fishhooks.

"How many!" said Violet. "I thought fishhooks were all alike."

"Not at all," Henry told her. "There are different hooks for different fish."

"What are those?" Violet pointed at a display of bright-colored fishing flies. "They look like insects made of feathers."

"They are called flies," the man who had the exhibit told Violet. "They are made to look like little insects, so the fish snap at them. Only now the river is spoiled by the paint factory. The pollution kills the fish."

Violet read the names of some of the flies, "Gray Ghost, Silver Doctor, Royal Coachman."

"There's a hook inside each one," said Henry.

An old man looking at the exhibit said, "I remember when you could catch fish by just dropping a line in the water. It's not that way anymore."

The man who had explained the fish flies to Violet nodded. "Yep. Every factory pours dirty water into the rivers. It's time to stop them! That's what the meeting is about tomorrow night—how to save our river."

Benny tried to think who else had spoken of a meeting tomorrow. Then he remembered. The boys on the bus!

"Let's go somewhere else," said Violet quickly. She didn't want to think about hooks in fish.

The Aldens went over to the pottery display. A girl was spinning her potter's wheel. She had just finished making a vase out of clay. Now she was making a design on the vase with a small wooden tool. As the vase whirled around on the wheel, the girl pressed the tool against the side of the vase. The tool made a perfect ring around the vase. Then another and another.

It was so fascinating to watch that Violet forgot all about the fishhooks.

Jessie turned to the others and said, "Now we can go see the clock. The big crowd is gone."

After Henry had looked at the clock he said, "It's hard to believe a boy invented this clock. It's clever the way it's made. The boy must be a genius."

Jessie began to smile. "Look at this eggbeater," she said. "It cleans itself! I always hate to wash an eggbeater. The egg is hard to wash off."

Benny said, "Come on. I see a good wildlife exhibit. Let's see what it's about."

The Aldens found there were drawings of birds, insects, and small animals. There were pots of wild plants and a bunch of wild flowers.

"Look at this," said Henry. "Now whoever thought of this is very clever."

Jessie looked at the card. "It says there are one hundred plants growing in this square—only one square yard of earth."

"You can see the square was taken from the earth just as it was, with nothing planted on purpose," remarked Benny.

Violet said, "Here is sour sorrel and wood sorrel, and white, pink, and red clover."

Jessie went on, fascinated with all the little plants, "Here is a yellow five-finger and chickweed and a strawberry plant."

"And a buttercup," said Benny. "I wonder who put this exhibit together?"

Then suddenly the Aldens saw the boy who was in charge of the wild flower exhibit. It was the older boy who had caught the bus from Plainville Junction —the very one Frank had ordered out of the bus station! He was busy explaining something to some people who were interested in the exhibit.

"Yes," he said, "we took a piece of land down by the river and put up stakes three feet apart to make a square. Then we counted all the different plants inside the square."

A woman asked, "You found all these different plants in that small space?"

The boy nodded. "We want to show what's lost when something like the paint factory spoils wild land." He looked right at the Aldens when he said that as if he thought they were going to spoil the land.

"That's a good exhibit, but that boy is not at all

friendly," Jessie said. "Let's move on."

The Aldens walked over to a collection of matchbook covers. Violet said, "I guess people collect anything. There are matchbooks from every state and some foreign countries."

"And here's a collection of pins," said Jessie. "Imagine collecting pins!"

Violet replied, "They are a good thing to collect because they don't take up much room."

Henry called Benny over to see model planes. Then Benny caught sight of an ice cream stand. "Let's have ice cream cones," he said. "I always choose chocolate."

"How can you be hungry after all that lunch?" Jessie asked.

"Always room for an ice cream cone," returned Benny.

"I wouldn't mind one myself," said Henry, feeling for his wallet.

Soon all the Aldens were enjoying ice cream cones. "Let's see that exhibit," said Benny, pointing to a display set up in the corner. "The sign says 'Pickett's Perfect Paints.' Look at the crowd!"

As they started over, Benny frowned. Pickett's Paints—that was the name on the envelope he had handed Frank. The Oakdale bus driver had given Frank a package for the Pickett factory.

The exhibit was interesting and bright. There were little toy houses painted in different colors. There were pieces of wood painted with Pickett paints and left out in the sun to weather. They showed how well the paint lasted and how bright it stayed.

The man in charge of the exhibit was trying to show how paint was made. He explained what made blue paint blue and red paint red.

A woman in the crowd said, "Mr. Pickett, just listen to me!"

So this was Mr. Pickett, the Aldens thought.

The woman continued. "I don't care what you put in your paints. Your factory is pouring all that horrible waste into a public river. It isn't your river. It belongs to the town."

"It's our river," a girl said.

An old man asked, "Where are the fish? We used to get fine fish from the river. And have a good time fishing, too."

A boy said, "Your old factory smells up the country for miles."

But a young man said, "Give Mr. Pickett a chance to talk. He knows his business. A big factory can be good for people around here."

Mr. Pickett looked happy to see at least one friendly face. He said, "Yes! I have a hundred workers in my paint factory. That means they earn money to take care of a hundred families. It means money to spend. I pay taxes for your schools. I'm a good neighbor to all of you!"

Suddenly there was a noise and everyone looked around to see what was happening. Some people began to laugh. Others shouted, "Go home!"

The Aldens stood on tiptoe to see what the excitement was about. It was a surprise. The two boys from Plainville Junction were pushing through the crowd toward the paint exhibit. They were waving signs.

One sign said, "SAVE OUR RIVER. DON'T POLLUTE!" The other read "NATURE IS BETTER THAN PAINT."

Some men and women clapped. Someone said,

"Those boys are brave to do that. I wouldn't have dared do anything like that."

Mr. Pickett stared at the boys and their signs. Benny wondered if he knew who they were. The boys never looked right at him. They waved their signs back and forth.

"Not fair! Not fair!" Mr. Pickett shouted angrily. "You can't picket me!"

For a minute it looked as if the paint exhibit was going to be smashed. The man in charge of the hobby fair came running over.

"All right!" the manager shouted. "Some of you want Mr. Pickett's factory. Some of you don't. This isn't the place to decide. Come to the town meeting tomorrow night, right here in the town hall. That's the place to discuss it. You boys—take those signs and get out. I will not have trouble here."

The boys did not argue. Perhaps they had done what they wanted to do. They had started people talking about the river.

The Aldens spent another hour looking around at the exhibits. At last Jessie asked, "When does the bus leave, Henry? We don't want to miss it."

Henry said, "We can spend half an hour here and still have time to get the bus. Where's Benny?"

"He was here a minute ago," Violet said. "Oh, there he is, over there with the manager."

"I'm glad you came all the way from Greenfield to see our hobby fair," the manager was saying to Benny. "It was too bad about that fuss around Mr. Pickett's exhibit."

Benny asked, "Who are those boys who wanted to picket Mr. Pickett?"

"Oh, everyone knows Jud and Troy. That's what makes it so bad. You saw their wildlife exhibit. I'll have to say they are smart boys."

"We saw them first at the bus station at Plainville Junction," Benny said.

"Yes, I imagine that is where you'd meet them," the manager said. "If they were my boys, I'd have something to say to them. They may be right, but they shouldn't act like that. Mr. Pickett has a right to show what he makes."

"You said something about a meeting tomorrow," Benny said.

"Yes, the voters of Plainville Township are going

to meet here at the Oakdale town hall. Posters announced the meeting ten days ago. It will be a regular town meeting. Mr. Pickett is coming. People want to ask him about his plans. He wants to buy more land. He says he needs a parking lot. He put his paint factory out there in the country because he needed the water and he didn't think anyone would care."

"But people do care, I guess," said Benny. "Can they stop him?"

The manager said, "Well, yes, I guess they can. But I don't know if that's what most people want to do. His business is good for Oakdale, and Oakdale is part of Plainville Township."

"Benny, time to go!" Jessie called.

Smiling at the manager, Benny said quickly, "I'm Benny Alden. Perhaps you know my grandfather, Mr. James Alden."

"I do indeed," said the manager. "He has a smart grandson, I see that."

Benny ran to catch up with Henry. "That was a great fair," he said. "I'm glad we came. It turned out to be exciting!"

CHAPTER 6

What Did Happen?

The bus for Greenfield was right on time. Quite a few people got on the bus. A man asked the driver, "You stop at the junction, don't you?"

"That's right," the driver said. "I'll call out the name when we get there."

"But you just stop there to let passengers off, don't

you?" a man asked. "You just go right along to Greenfield?"

"Right," said the driver.

Then Benny got on.

"Good evening," the driver said pleasantly to Benny. It was the same driver who had taken them from Plainville Junction to Oakdale. "Did you have a good time at the fair?" Everyone seemed to speak to Benny.

"Oh, swell," replied Benny. "You ought to go."

"I've been there," said the driver. "I go every year. And I always see something new."

The Aldens found seats in the middle of the bus. Jessie and Violet sat near each other. Benny took a seat in front of Violet. Henry found an empty seat across the aisle. The bus was not crowded.

Benny half expected to see the two boys—Jud and Troy—catch the bus. But they were nowhere to be seen.

While Henry pushed the back of his seat into a comfortable position, Benny said, "I'm glad we don't have to change buses at Plainville Junction. I don't want to wait there again."

"I wonder if the tree across the road to the bridge has been moved," Henry said, settling back. "That could make us late."

"It's probably been pulled out of the way long ago," answered Benny. "The road crews are pretty fast. Do you think we'll see Frank around the bus station? I'd like to say hello."

Henry shrugged. "There won't be time to go in the station. This bus goes right through. It will just stop to let passengers off and pick up anyone who's waiting."

"Too bad," Benny said. "I'm hungry. I'd like to go in the bus station and get one of Frank's good doughnuts."

Henry gave a big yawn. He shut his eyes and was soon asleep.

Benny stared out of the bus window. He liked the countryside. He thought about the storm. Except for the trees near Frank's bus station, it had not done much damage.

Benny, too, must have fallen asleep, for the next thing he knew, the driver was calling out, "Plainville Junction!"

"Remember I'm getting off," the man called. "I've got these shopping bags, and I can't move fast."

The driver laughed. "Sure, I'll give you a hand. Just stay in your seat until we get there."

The big bus bumped off the highway and stopped in front of the bus station. Benny, who was sitting next to the window, stared out. Suddenly he poked Henry.

"Wake up, Henry!" Benny said excitedly. "Something's going on at the bus station."

"What? Where?" asked Henry. Now he was wide awake and leaning forward to look out of the window, too.

Something was going on, but it was hard to tell what it was.

Three men with lunch boxes were waiting for the bus. Someone had given each of them a pink paper.

Then the Aldens saw who was passing out the papers. The two boys, Jud and Troy, were waving more papers and saying something.

The Aldens could not hear because the bus windows were closed. But they could guess the boys wanted the men to read the papers.

Suddenly everyone—the men and the boys—looked around behind them.

The door of a large car opened and out stepped a man who was plainly very angry. He did not turn off his motor or shut the door. Instead he made a quick rush at Jud and Troy.

The boys were startled. The man grabbed the papers from the boys' hands. He tore the sheets in half and threw them on the ground.

Everyone gasped.

While the men waiting for the bus edged out of the way and the people on the bus watched, something strange happened.

The man pointed at his car and plainly said "Get in!" to the boys. He pushed them in front of him and into the back seat of the car. He slammed the door, jumped in himself, and with a screech of tires pulled away from the bus station.

No one had had time to do a thing.

"Well!" said Benny. "What's going on?"

Violet leaned forward and whispered, "You—you don't think the boys were kidnapped, do you? It all happened so fast."

"No, I don't think so," Henry answered. "The two boys seemed to know the man."

Now Benny noticed Frank standing on the bus station steps, his hands on his hips. He looked as surprised as everyone else. But he did not rush to help Jud or Troy. Like the men, he just watched.

The bus driver was impatient. He called out, "All aboard! Let's go. I'm late already." The men with their lunch boxes and sheets of paper got on, not saying a word.

The driver released the brake, turned the bus, and was out on the highway. Looking back, Benny just had time to see Frank pick up the torn papers.

All kinds of questions buzzed around in Benny's head and Henry's too. Benny felt that if he could just see one of those papers, he might find some answers.

The three men who had just gotten on the bus were sitting in the back. Benny couldn't call out to them. He couldn't even turn around enough to see if the men were reading the pink papers.

"Who was that man?" Henry asked Benny. "I feel sure I've seen him."

"Me, too," Benny said. "Now where? Greenfield? No, I don't think so."

The boys said nothing for a minute, and then Benny said, "Wait, I know! It was at the hobby fair this afternoon. How could I have been so stupid? That was Mr. Pickett. Mr. Pickett of the paint factory. I'm sure of it!"

"You're right, you're absolutely right," Henry exclaimed. "Of course it was Mr. Pickett. His factory is near the bus station. He must turn off the highway there."

"Or was he coming to see Frank?" Benny suggested.

"I don't know," Henry answered. "There was that letter he sent Frank . . ."

"He was mad at Jud and Troy. That's sure," Benny said thoughtfully. "Wow! I wouldn't want someone to come after me that way!"

Henry nodded. "You know, Ben, there is something funny going on. The boys went with him. They didn't try to escape or run away."

"That's right," Benny agreed. "They looked mad, too. And surprised."

"Well, they couldn't have been too surprised," Henry said. "After all, they did wave those signs against the paint factory in front of Mr. Pickett at the hobby fair. They knew they made him mad then. They didn't seem to care too much if they did make him mad."

"There's something else I don't understand," Benny said after a moment. "Frank just watched. He didn't help the boys. And he didn't help Mr. Pickett. Wouldn't you think he'd be on one side or the other?"

"You're right, Benny," said Henry. "Nobody did a thing. That's something to think about."

The bus rolled along and Benny and Henry stared out of the window. They were quiet. Benny was thinking again about the sheets of paper being passed out. If he could just get one . . .

"East Greenfield," the bus driver announced. The three men who had gotten on the bus at Plainville Junction came forward.

"Another day gone," the driver said as he opened the bus door. "Well, see you tomorrow. Take care now."

"So long," the men said. One of them waved.

Benny looked at Henry. "You know, those men must work at Pickett's factory. I never thought of that before."

"Sure," Henry agreed. "They must catch this bus home from work every day. The driver knows them."

"I wonder what they thought about how Mr. Pickett acted," Benny said. Then he felt a gentle touch on his sleeve.

It was Violet. She pushed a printed paper around the back of his seat so that no one else would notice.

"One of the men who rode on the bus threw this down as he got ready to get off," Violet whispered.

The paper was folded over several times. Benny opened it and read "Town Meeting."

Underneath there was a message printed by hand. It read: "Come and save the river. It is not too late. You can help."

"So!" Benny exclaimed. "Jud and Troy don't give up. They want Mr. Pickett's workers to vote against him at the town meeting. And Mr. Pickett is their boss. Vote against your own boss. How about that!"

"It looks that way," Henry said. "I'd like to know what's going on now. Why did Mr. Pickett push the boys into his car? I suppose he tried to scare them some way."

"Probably turned them over to their parents," Benny said. "I'll bet there was trouble."

"I don't think they'll have a chance to go to the town meeting tomorrow," Henry said.

"Not a chance," Benny agreed.

"Greenfield!" the driver called out. The Aldens jumped down from the bus, happy to get home.

"Dinner!" exclaimed Benny. "Am I starved! Let's go!"

When he undressed for bed that night, Benny thought about Jud and Troy and all that had happened on this one day.

"I wonder if we'll read in the newspaper what happened at the town meeting," he said to himself. "I'd like to know what Mr. Pickett really did with Jud and Troy. Too bad—perhaps I'll never know."

As he was falling asleep, Benny thought, "I'd just like to know how it all comes out. I'll have to think about it . . . tomorrow." But he was too sleepy to go on.

CHAPTER 7

The Snooper

The next morning Benny lay in bed wondering what excuse he could give to get back to the bus station. He couldn't think of anything.

He wondered what had happened to Jud and Troy after Mr. Pickett had driven off with them. Would they get to the town meeting? What were they planning to do?

Benny wondered about Frank, too. Frank had said someone was too big for him to fight. What did that mean? He was a chemist. Maybe he had a new kind of paint he wanted Mr. Pickett to make.

There was a lot going on that Benny did not understand. He wanted to listen, to ask questions, maybe to help.

Then Benny thought, "Our raincoats! We left our raincoats at the bus station. Hooray!"

He dressed quickly for breakfast. But to his surprise he found everyone dressed and eating breakfast, too.

Benny began, "Henry, guess what? We forgot—"

"Our raincoats," finished Henry. "We were just talking about that. We'll have to go back and get them."

"We should call Frank before we start off," Jessie suggested. "We have to be sure that our raincoats are still at the bus station."

The telephone lines had been repaired after the big storm. Soon Benny was speaking to Frank on the telephone.

"Yes," Frank told him. The raincoats were there.

He was wondering if he should mail them to the Aldens.

"Oh, no," Benny said. "That's too much trouble. My big brother Henry can drive over today and get them. Will this morning be all right?"

To Benny's surprise, Frank didn't like that idea at all. He said he had planned to be away from the station for two hours.

"I'm sorry," Benny said. He didn't want Frank to be angry with the Aldens. "We don't want to be any bother. We can come later and get our raincoats."

This time Frank agreed.

Benny hung up the telephone and turned around to the others. He said, "I don't understand Frank at all. You'd think he'd be glad to have us get the raincoats. I don't think he wants us to come at all. He sounds as if—as if he's hiding something. I wonder what's going on."

"Perhaps he wants to go fishing," Jessie suggested. "I don't think the bus station keeps him very busy."

Benny shook his head. "Why wouldn't he say he's going fishing? There's nothing wrong with that. We would understand."

Henry had been thinking. He said, "There is that big town meeting about the paint factory tonight. I wonder if Frank plans to go."

"Remember how we saw Mr. Pickett at the bus station last night," Benny said. "Maybe he came to see Frank. It was an accident he caught the boys passing out those papers."

"Frank doesn't trust those boys," Jessie said. "He likes to keep his own secrets."

Benny agreed. "You remember how he asked what in the world we were doing when he came back after the storm and saw the chair under the shelf. He thought we were fussing around with his things. Really, we were wrong. We had no right to look at Frank's things, even if we didn't touch them."

"Do you think those chemistry books have anything to do with this mystery?" asked Jessie.

"Well, we won't find out what's going on while we sit here," Henry said. "We've never even seen Mr. Pickett's paint factory. Maybe we should visit it and then get our raincoats from Frank."

"Good idea," said Benny. "Let's go."

It was a fine summer day. The storm of yesterday

seemed like a bad dream. The Aldens were glad to have an excuse to drive out in the country and visit the bus station again.

"I'm glad we decided to do something," Violet said. "I can't stay at home on a day like this."

"Neither can I," said Benny, laughing.

Henry did not follow the road the bus took to Plainville Junction. He chose a back road that crossed the red bridge near the bus station.

"It is a lovely river," Jessie said. "Grandfather called this country empty. But it isn't really. Remember Jud and Troy's wildlife exhibit at the fair? I never knew so many kinds of plants and animals could be found in such a little space."

Suddenly they noticed a flight of wild ducks overhead. The ducks all dropped down into the river and dived to the bottom to find food. However, they came up right away, flapped their wet wings, and flew up the river, flying very low.

"Honk! Honk!" they cried.

Jessie said, "Look at that! The river is spoiled. The ducks can't find food. I hope the chemicals won't hurt them."

"I don't think they stayed long enough," said Henry. "Just look at that triangle of ducks. They always follow the leader."

All the ducks except the leader were honking. Then all at once they stopped and the leader honked all alone. "Honk! Honk! Honk!"

Benny laughed and said, "The leader keeps saying, 'Well, if you all want to pass, go on!' "

Henry looked up the road toward the bus station. He slowed down suddenly. He saw a bright-colored pickup truck parked beside the road near the station. He could just make out the words "Pickett's Perfect Paints" on the back of the truck.

Benny saw the truck, too. "Looks as if Frank has company," he said. "Do you think that's why he didn't want us to come?"

"I don't know," Henry said. "Might be. I'll drive past the station slowly. Let's see if it looks closed."

Violet could see the bus station better than the others.

"There's a card in the window," Violet reported. "It says 'Buy tickets on bus.' I think the station is closed."

"That's funny," Benny said. "I'm sure I saw somebody going around the station."

"I'll park the car where it can't be seen from the station," Henry said. "Then we'll walk back and take a look around."

"Maybe someone's up to some mischief," Benny said. He thought about the weeds and the chemistry books. Did they have something to do with the paint factory? Or were they for something else? Perhaps someone from the paint factory wanted to find out.

The big trees along the road hid the Aldens as they walked toward the bus station. No one talked. They didn't know what to expect. Perhaps nothing at all was going on.

"Look!" whispered Benny, and he pulled Jessie out of sight behind a tree.

A man who moved like a gray shadow came around the small building. When the Aldens could see him better, they found he was wearing gray coveralls. It was a work uniform of some sort. A big paint can was stitched on the back of the suit.

Yes, it had to be somebody from the paint factory, Benny decided. Then he had an idea. Could it be

Mr. Pickett dressed up as a worker? What could he want?

The man stood on tiptoe and looked in the window at the side. He knocked gently against the glass. Was he planning to break it?

The stranger walked around to the front door. He tried to open it. The door was locked. He pushed. Then he used his shoulder, but the door did not open.

The Aldens watched from behind the trees. Suddenly the man seemed to give up. He turned around and sat down on the doorstep.

"What now?" Benny whispered.

The man felt in a pocket. He pulled out a piece of paper. Then he felt in other pockets until he found a pencil. He sat still for a moment, then he began to write.

CHAPTER 8

Tricked Twice

Not one of the Aldens moved. They watched the man on the bus station steps. What was he going to do?

Henry motioned to Jessie and Violet. He wanted them to stay where they were. He whispered to Benny, "Come with me."

Benny nodded and tiptoed behind Henry. The girls stayed where they were, out of sight.

Henry led Benny back toward their station wagon. He said in a low voice, "Let's see if we can find out what that man wants. If he's up to some harm, maybe we can learn what it is and tell Frank."

"If there's a good reason for his actions, then we won't have to worry," Benny said.

"Here's my idea," Henry went on. "We'll walk toward the bus station as if we want to catch a bus. When we get near the man, say something to me like, 'I thought we'd never find this bus station.' You know, stuff like that."

"OK," Benny said. "Let's go. I hope he hasn't gone."

"I'm sure he hasn't. We'd hear the truck start," Henry said.

The boys walked along quickly. They tried to act as if they were not doing anything unusual.

As they came near the bus station they saw the man on the steps, stooping down near the door. They couldn't tell what he was doing.

Benny said loudly, "Am I glad to see the bus station! My feet hurt."

Jessie, hidden behind a tree, nearly laughed aloud.

"I hope we haven't missed the bus," Henry said.

"You haven't," said the man on the steps, and Benny jumped.

"You're—you're sure?" he asked.

"Naw, you haven't missed it," the man said. "The fellow who keeps this station has it all closed up. Nobody at all around."

Henry said, "But we have to buy tickets."

"Read the sign," the man said. "You buy your tickets on the bus. Where you want to go?"

"Greenfield," Benny said quickly.

"You got a long wait. No bus until this afternoon. You been visiting around here?"

Benny swallowed. He was supposed to be asking the questions, not answering them. He looked over at Henry.

"We were visiting Jud and Troy," Henry said. Those were the only names he knew of anyone nearby.

"Down on the river? What did their dad do to them after they passed out those papers last night?"

Henry had to think fast. He didn't know what had happened to the boys. So he just said, "They got in trouble, all right. Did you come to the bus station for something?"

The man shrugged. "I told the foreman at the plant it wouldn't do any good. But he wanted me to come to see if Frank was around. One of the machines broke and we need a new part to fix it. The part was supposed to come on the bus yesterday. You can send packages on the bus, you know. Faster than the mail."

"Did Frank have the package?" Henry asked.

"How do I know? Frank isn't here. I just pushed a note under the door. I'll come back later for it. Got to get back to work now. Tell Frank hello for me—if you see him."

"For you?" Henry asked.

"Yeah, tell him Bill was here. Have a good wait."

The workman walked down the steps and headed for the truck.

When the truck was out of sight Henry and Benny began to laugh.

"You never had a chance to find out a thing," Henry told Benny. "Bill was asking all the questions."

Jessie and Violet came running up. "What was going on?" asked Jessie. "Do you think the man was snooping around?"

"He wanted a package that came on the bus," Benny said. "That was all. I guess he thought he'd take it if he could get in. It's something to fix some machinery at the paint factory."

"What shall we do now?" Violet asked. "Wait for Frank here?"

"We know he isn't in the station, that's one thing sure," Benny said.

"Why not look for Frank?" Violet asked. "I don't feel like waiting here."

"Not enough excitement?" Henry asked, teasing Violet a little. "All right, let me get the car."

Jessie said, "Oh, Henry, put the car behind the bus station. Let's walk. His house is about a mile away, right on the river. We can't miss it."

The Aldens left their car at the bus station. They locked it and set off for the river.

"We have to go single file," Henry said. "I'll go first, and Benny, you bring up the rear."

There was a narrow, well-worn path along the

river. Benny said, "We should see some fishermen along here. It's just the kind of day for fishermen. Where are they?"

Violet stopped and pointed to a dark streak in the middle of the stream. "Do you see where the water is so dirty?" she asked. "I wonder what makes that."

"Ugh," Benny said. "I wouldn't want to swim here."

Henry said, "I think the paint factory waste makes the whole river look different."

They walked along until they thought they must be near Frank's house.

"Maybe we should look around and not just walk up and bang on Frank's door," Benny suggested.

The others agreed. So when they saw a boat pulled up on the shore and the roof of a small house behind some trees, they stopped.

"That has to be Frank's house. I see a birdhouse in one of the trees," said Jessie.

There was a little breeze. Jessie sniffed, then she held her nose. "I forgot about that queer smell at the bus station yesterday. Now I smell it again."

"Look over there," said Benny, pointing. "See that

big chimney? I think we've found Frank's house and the paint factory, too."

As he spoke, a truck passed the Aldens on the road above the riverbank. It was going to the factory.

"What do we do now?" Jessie asked. She was standing on the path. Bushes and tall grass nearly hid the trail.

There was a rustling sound. A twig snapped.

"Shhh!" Henry whispered. "Get down." He was sure he had seen someone or something move in the tall grass nearby.

The Aldens dropped down behind Henry. No one said a word. They waited.

"Caught you!" a voice said softly.

"Yeah, caught you!" a second voice said. "What do you want here?"

Slowly the Aldens stood up. The voices belonged to Jud and Troy. The boys scowled at the Aldens.

"We were looking for Frank," Benny said, no longer surprised. "Anything wrong with that?"

"Sneaking around is a funny way to look for someone," Jud declared. "Are you spying on Frank or something?"

"That's stupid," Henry said. He felt angry at the boys for suspecting anything like that. "We never met Frank until yesterday. We forgot our raincoats and came back to save Frank the trouble of mailing a package."

"Yeah?" Troy asked. "Do you believe that, Jud?" He turned to his brother.

Jud looked at the Aldens. "I kind of believe it," he said slowly. "Four people are too many to take along if you're up to something wrong."

Jessie said, "We left our raincoats at the bus station yesterday. We came to get them. The station was locked, so we started to look for Frank."

"I guess you're OK," Jud said. "You'll find Frank down by the river." And he and Troy climbed up to the road and disappeared.

"Those boys scared me for a minute," Violet said. "Do you think they were spying on Frank?"

"Or spying *for* him?" asked Benny. "I'm all mixed up."

"Let's find Frank anyway," Henry decided.

They had not gone far down the path when Violet called, "I see him!"

Frank was lying on the riverbank, pulling something out of the water. He looked around and saw the Aldens.

Jessie said quickly, "We got here early. We just thought we'd come and find you." She held her breath. Would he be angry?

"I'm glad you did," answered Frank. "You are just in time to see what I found." He lifted a large dead fish as he spoke. "It was right here floating upside down in the river. Too bad."

The Aldens looked at the fish. "That would have made a big dinner for someone," said Jessie.

"Me," said Frank. "I used to sit here and fish and have a good time by myself. Sometimes I caught a fish in ten minutes. Now every fish is dead and it's not fun even being on the river in a boat. Pollution has ruined the river."

"What are you going to do with that dead fish?" Benny asked.

Frank gave a queer laugh. "I think I have a special use for it. It will make a real surprise for someone." He wrapped the fish in paper as he spoke. "I'll drive you back to the bus station. Then you can get your raincoats."

CHAPTER 9

Frank's Problem

Frank put the dead fish in the trunk of his car. He locked the door of his house, then he got in the driver's seat. The Aldens slid in, with Benny and Henry sitting in front with Frank.

"I'm glad we don't have the fish with us," Violet whispered to Jessie.

They were soon at the bus station and Frank was unlocking the door. He found Bill's note and put it with the package that had come on the bus.

"If I close up like this in the morning, I don't miss much business," he said. "Too late for breakfast and too early for lunch."

The Aldens had followed Frank into the station. They saw the sun shining in the clean windows. The flowers in the pots on the sills were bright and gay. Frank opened a window and the room was filled with a bird song.

Frank looked around as if the station was his own little kingdom. He said, "Sit down, kids, and let me tell you something. I think you'll understand, and I need to talk to someone."

The Aldens sat down quietly and waited. Frank was a puzzling person. He was angry one minute and gentle the next.

Frank reached down and pulled out the envelope Benny had handed him yesterday. He unfolded the letter.

He began, "You saw the chimney of the paint factory when you came to find me. The factory is right there on the river around a little bend from me. You might say it's my neighbor."

"We smelled it, too," Benny said.

"You can say that again," said Henry.

"I will," said Benny. "We smelled it, too."

Frank laughed. "That's just part of the problem. I don't like it, but that isn't the worst of it."

Frank got up and put the letter down. He pulled out a big notebook. Opening it, he said, "I think you've guessed that maybe I'm not just a lunch-counter man and bus station keeper. I'm a chemist. I like living in a quiet place like this. I'm interested in growing plants without using chemicals. I like birds and wild animals. That's why I'm here."

"We understand," Violet said quietly.

"Everything was fine until this Mr. Pickett came along and built his paint factory. There was no way to stop him. He bought the land. He could do what he liked out here in the country. He didn't expect to bother anyone."

"He can spoil the river and no one will care?" Henry asked. "Is that what he thinks?"

"Yes," Frank said. "But he is wrong. He has to

be stopped. But how? That's the question."

Frank dropped his head in his hands. Then he went on quietly, "I did some experiments to show how the water from the factory pollutes the river. The chemicals are carried in the water. They kill fish and water plants. I thought that if I showed this notebook about my experiments to Mr. Pickett he would stop polluting."

"But that didn't work?" Benny asked.

Frank shook his head. "Mr. Pickett just said it was too bad, but lots of people have jobs at his factory. It was too late to build somewhere else."

Benny looked angry. "Build somewhere else? Pollute somewhere else? That's no answer."

"That's what I said," Frank continued. "I told him that there are laws to stop pollution. He told me I was a troublemaker. He said he'd get rid of me."

"How?" asked Jessie.

"Easy enough, I guess," Frank said. "Mr. Pickett bought all the land along the river. That means all the land around my house and garden. If he likes, he can keep me from getting to my house. That's what he told me."

"That's not fair!" Henry said. "There must be some way to stop him."

Frank said, "It takes money. I'd have to go to court. Anyway, now he has a new idea. He wants to buy my house and garden to make into a parking lot for the factory workers. Imagine! Tear down my house. Cover my garden with blacktop. That's what his letter to me was about. I'm not rich. I can't fight him."

The Aldens looked at each other. Benny decided to ask another question. "What about Jud and Troy?"

"Yes," Henry added. "We saw them giving out papers at the bus station when our bus stopped yesterday."

Frank gave his angry short laugh again. "Oh, yes! They think they can change things. They tried to show how important the river is to wildlife. Older people don't pay attention to boys. Then they tried to line up some of the workers against the paint factory. You saw how that worked out."

"Not at all," Jessie said.

"Yesterday in Oakdale we heard about the town meeting tonight," Henry said. "We know it's about Mr. Pickett's factory and the way it's polluting the river. Are you going?"

"I'm going," Frank answered. Then he shook his head. "But I don't think there'll be much of a crowd.

Mr. Pickett and his workers and friends will be there. Nobody will do anything."

Jessie said, "It sounded to us as if a lot of people want to save the river, just as you do. You're not alone. You have to believe that."

For a minute Frank did not say anything. Then he looked right at the Aldens. "That *is* good news. Do you know what I was going to do? I was going to take that dead fish to the town meeting and pass it around among the people. It was a stupid idea, but I was angry enough to do it."

Benny liked the idea. He knew just how angry Frank felt. He said, "I don't think that would be such a bad idea. It would show the townspeople just how bad the river is."

Frank said, "If what you say is true and a lot of people really care, maybe we *can* save the river."

Benny said in a rush, "I know we're outsiders. But maybe we can help, too."

"How?" asked Frank, looking surprised.

"Our grandfather has plastics factories. Maybe you have heard of him. He is Mr. James Alden. His factories don't pollute any rivers. They don't make any bad smells either. Let's see if Grandfather will come to the town meeting. He's a businessman. Perhaps he can talk to Mr. Pickett."

Frank thought for a moment. Then he said, "It's worth trying. Will he come?"

Benny said, "Let me call him right now. We Aldens always like to do things in a hurry!"

CHAPTER 10

Benny Guesses

As the Aldens drove up to the town hall in Oakdale Benny exclaimed, "Look at the crowd! I never thought so many people would come to a town meeting."

Grandfather smiled. He had been at town meetings before.

"Do you see Frank anywhere?" Jessie asked. "I hope he comes early and meets Grandfather."

Henry parked the car behind the truck from the paint factory. Someone had crossed out the last letter T on the sign. Now it read "Pickett's Perfect Pain."

Henry started to laugh, then he stopped. "There are some people around here who really want to get rid of Mr. Pickett and his factory," he said.

"I hope there won't be any trouble at the town meeting," Jessie said. "People are excited."

"There's Frank," Benny called, waving to him. "I don't think he brought the dead fish. He has no bundle under his arm."

After Frank and Mr. Alden had met, the two men stood and talked in quiet voices. People walking into the town hall looked curiously at them.

Benny heard a woman say, "We'll get the state inspectors to close Mr. Pickett's factory. He can't get away with spoiling our river."

"Wait a minute," a man said. "I work for Mr. Pickett. I need a job. Don't try to take work away from me! I don't want the factory closed."

"There's Mr. Pickett," Violet whispered.

Mr. Pickett walked along quickly. Several men were with him. They did not look at Frank or Mr. Alden.

"I thought we'd see Jud and Troy," Benny said, looking around. "They're late."

"They won't be coming," Frank said. "They are against the paint factory. It wouldn't surprise me if their father has them locked up at home."

"Locked up!" Benny exclaimed. "They didn't do anything that bad."

"You can try telling their father that," Frank said.

Benny and Violet went over toward the town hall. The others stood, still talking. Benny thought Grandfather looked like an old general planning for a battle. And maybe it would be a battle—there was a lot of excitement as people gathered.

Suddenly Benny stopped Violet and said, "Look over there! Frank's wrong. Here they come."

"Who? Where?" Violet asked.

"Jud and Troy! They're locking their bikes up at the rack over there."

"Do you think they rode into Oakdale from Plainville Junction?" Violet asked. "That's a long ride."

"It is," Benny agreed. "I guess they really wanted to get here. I hope they aren't going to start any trouble. It would be easy to get this crowd angry."

Then Benny heard a voice he knew. It was Troy's. He was with Jud.

Troy was saying, "We couldn't leave until Dad was gone. And if we walk into the meeting after it has started, everyone will stare at us."

"You don't see Dad outside, do you?" Jud asked. "How about his friends?" He sounded worried. Then he saw the Aldens.

"Look who's here!" he exclaimed. "Did you forget something again?"

"Yeah, you're outsiders. What are you doing here?" Troy asked.

"We're with Frank," Benny said. He didn't see why he had to explain anything to these boys.

"With Frank?" Jud asked. He looked around then and saw Frank and the other Aldens coming into the building, too.

"Who's that with you?" Troy asked.

"That's my grandfather," Benny answered. "He has some ideas that can help save the river."

"He does?" Troy asked, surprised. "Do you think my dad will listen?"

"Boy, I wish he would," Jud said. "I really wish he would."

"We've tried everything we can think of," Troy said. "Dad says there isn't anything he can do. He doesn't want the river spoiled. But he thinks he can't do anything about it."

The town meeting was about to begin. The last people who had been standing outside were beginning to come in.

"Come on," Jud said to his brother, "I don't want Frank to see us. Let's slip in and get some seats where Dad won't see us."

The boys disappeared, leaving Benny standing there. He saw his family and Frank starting toward the hall entrance.

Still Benny stood in the one spot. He was putting a lot of ideas together. Who was Jud and Troy's father? Benny thought he knew—should he tell the others? Maybe not. They'd find out soon enough, he felt.

Inside the hall, chairs were set up in rows. There

was an aisle down the middle. A long table at the front was for the township officers.

All Mr. Pickett's friends and workers sat together on one side. The persons who wanted to save the river filled the seats on the other side of the aisle. Up in front, the township officers took their places.

The big clock showed exactly eight o'clock. The crowd grew quiet as the moderator called the meeting to order. He explained why everyone had been asked to come. He said he hoped some way could be found to save the river. He asked everyone to take turns in speaking.

First, Mr. Pickett stood up to tell how his new factory helped Plainview Township. He pointed out that people needed jobs. He believed workers needed something useful, like good paint, to make. When he said Pickett's Perfect Paint was the best, some of the people behind him clapped.

The moderator said, "Let's hear from that lady from Oakdale."

The woman rose and said, "We need new factories. We need work so that people can buy things at our stores. But we don't want our river spoiled.

People are important. So is nature. Isn't there some way we can have jobs and save the river too?"

Men and women on both sides of the hall clapped.

Benny twisted around to see if he could find Jud and Troy in the audience. He finally saw them sitting toward the back. They had slid down in their seats as if they didn't want anyone to recognize them. Benny didn't blame them. Not if his guess was right.

A man who introduced himself as a teacher spoke next. He told how the river had changed since the factory had been built.

"Mr. Pickett may make good paint, but he is ruining our river," he declared. "We can't swim in it. We can't fish in it. And all because one man pours dirty water from his factory into it. I say Mr. Pickett's factory should be closed. We can do it!"

"Agree! Agree!" many people called out.

Mr. Pickett jumped to his feet. "You can't do that!" he cried. "You can't close my factory. I have put a lot of money in my business. Who needs fish from the river? You can buy fish at the market the way I do." Then he sat down.

Suddenly a lot of angry voices began to fill the

hall. It was impossible to tell what was being said.

The man in charge of the meeting called out, "Order! Order! Let one person speak at a time."

Frank raised his hand to show that he had something to say.

Benny was sorry not to see the bundle of fish in his hand. "Too bad," he said to Henry. "That fish would have been a good piece of evidence."

To everyone's surprise, Frank went to a table and opened a drawer. He took out a newspaper bundle.

"You don't have to touch this," Frank said to the people. "But I assure you it is a fresh dead fish."

"Fresh dead fish," everyone murmured, half laughing.

"It's fresh," Frank went on, "because it hasn't been dead long. Just this afternoon this fish was swimming in our river. Then I saw him stop swimming and float to the top. I picked him up. You can find a fish like this almost any time, poisoned by waste from the paint factory."

"That's a fine new piece of evidence," called a teen-ager from the front row.

"Just exactly what I said!" Benny whispered.

But Frank had not quite finished what he wanted to say. "I have called the factory a bad neighbor," he said. "And now Mr. Pickett wants to buy my house and land and make it into a parking lot."

"And you're going to sell him your land?" someone asked, sounding shocked.

"No!" Frank shouted. "I'm not selling. But I am hoping Mr. Pickett can become a good neighbor. If he makes some changes in his factory, I believe he can make paint and not spoil the river. Just spend some money, that's how!"

Mr. Pickett stood up. He looked at the men and women in the hall before speaking. Then he said, "I do want to be a good neighbor to Frank and to everyone. But who can show me how to run my factory and keep the river clean?"

"This gentleman over here can, I think," Frank answered and asked Grandfather to rise. "Mr. James Alden."

Everyone turned around to stare. Mr. Alden stood up and smiled. Then he walked over to Mr. Pickett and shook his hand.

"I have had some of the same troubles in my

plastics factories that you have had," he explained. "Bad odors. Polluted water. In my plants we have found a way to burn the bad-smelling gases before they go up the chimney. We need a great deal of water. But we use the same water over and over. Not a bit of dirty water empties into any river or sewer."

"None?" asked Mr. Pickett.

"None. The dirty water goes into big tanks. The dirt and pollution settle to the bottom of the tanks. Clean water rises to the top. It can be used again, and the tanks are cleaned out to hold more water."

Mr. Pickett was listening carefully.

Mr. Alden continued, "You probably have a dust problem in your factory, too. That's not bad for the river, but it is bad for your workers. We use a huge suction machine to pull the dust out of the air so that the air is safe to breathe."

The moderator asked, "Do I understand you, Mr. Alden? You say that Mr. Pickett's factory can make paint and be a better place to work, too?"

"Exactly," said Mr. Alden. "If Mr. Pickett agrees, I'll be glad to take him to my factories and show him what we do. My men will explain how the air and water are kept clean. I will be happy to talk with him about the business details."

Now everyone looked at Mr. Pickett. He spoke slowly. "Of course I know Mr. Alden's name. With his help I think I can make some changes." He smiled. "Then we'll have Pickett's Perfect Paint forever and a clean river, too!"

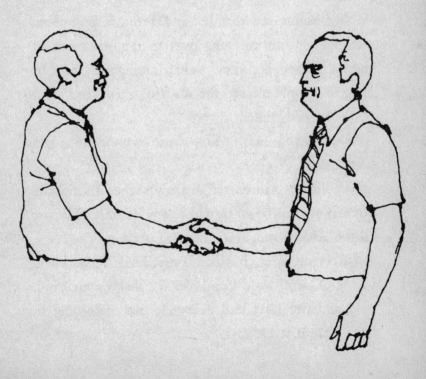

Everyone clapped. Benny turned around to see what Jud and Troy were doing. They were on their feet, clapping and edging toward the aisle. Were they going to slip out before the meeting was over?

The moderator called for order. He thanked everyone, then smiled and said, "If we work together, we can solve our problems. Meeting adjourned!"

Now Benny saw that Jud and Troy weren't going out. They were hurrying over to the other side of the hall. Suddenly they were running toward Mr. Pickett. People cleared the way for them, and some of the crowd smiled.

"Dad!" Jud said. "You were wonderful! You were great!"

Mr. Pickett had started to frown when he saw the boys. Now his frown turned to a wide smile. He saw all the Aldens and Frank coming over, too.

"Meet my sons, Jud and Troy," Mr. Pickett said to Mr. Alden. "And Frank, let me shake your hand. You and my boys and everyone else are going to have a clean river."

CHAPTER 11

Back to the Station

It was a beautiful summer night. When the meeting was over many people stopped to talk before starting their cars. There was a light wind, fresh and clean.

One man said, "This is the way it should always be. There should be clean air everywhere. I'm glad we had the meeting tonight."

An older man said, "It was time something was done. I don't know how the people living near the river have been able to stay there."

"My kids don't want to play outside," replied another man. "But we never dared to say anything to that Mr. Pickett. He's too powerful."

"Well that Mr. Alden isn't afraid," a woman said. "He got things straightened out in a hurry. But it was really Mr. Alden's grandchildren that gave Frank Timmons courage to face Mr. Pickett. I have a feeling that with Mr. Alden to help, it won't take much time to get the air fit to breathe."

The four grandchildren heard this with a smile as they watched the people drive away.

"I guess the public is with us," said Jessie. "What a surprise it was to learn that Jud and Troy were Mr. Pickett's sons!"

Frank said, "I guess I thought you knew."

Henry asked, "Did you call them troublemakers yesterday because they were Mr. Pickett's boys?"

Frank smiled. "Yes," he said. "Well, at first I thought that Mr. Pickett's own sons would of course be on his side. When I got to know Jud and Troy a little better, I liked them because they were interested in plants and animals. I knew they wanted their father to do something about his factory. But I didn't agree with what they were doing."

"Picketing their own father wasn't such a smart idea," Henry admitted.

"There was something else, too," Frank said. "I was having a lot of trouble with Mr. Pickett. He thought I was the troublemaker. He wanted to make me move away. It didn't help to have the boys around the station. It was bad, no matter how I looked at it."

"But now everything will be different, won't it?" asked Violet.

Benny looked around. The Aldens and Frank were the only people left standing in the moonlight in front of the town hall.

"Well," Mr. Alden said, "I think we must be leaving. Perhaps you can come along when my men come to talk with Mr. Pickett. A good chemist can be a real help."

"I'll be glad to," Frank said. "I've enjoyed meeting all of you."

"I guess this is good-bye then," Jessie said soberly.

"We're always saying good-bye to bus stations and islands and boxcars and things like that," Benny said with a laugh.

But the Aldens hadn't counted on what Frank would say next.

"Good-bye?" he said in a surprised voice. "I won't hear of it."

The Aldens looked at Frank. What was he thinking of now? They did not have to wait long to find out.

"Good-bye for tonight, maybe," Frank continued. "But I'd like you all to be my guests for a bus station dinner next Wednesday night. What do you say?"

"A bus station dinner!" Benny exclaimed. "Count me in! I never miss a dinner."

Everyone laughed so loud at what Benny said that Grandfather stepped over to see what all the noise was about.

"Guess what, Grandfather," Jessie said. "Frank has just invited us for a home-cooked dinner, served right at the bus station. Doesn't that sound like fun?"

"It certainly does," Mr. Alden replied with a

twinkle in his eye. "I almost forgot you were a cook, Frank. I always think of you as a clean-water man."

Frank laughed. "I have to be a cook to run a lunch counter at a bus station."

"Right," Mr. Alden said.

"*You'll* come for dinner, too, of course," Frank said to Grandfather. "After all, I owe you a great deal. Without your offering to show Mr. Pickett how you made your own factory safe, I might have lost my home. And the river might not have been saved."

"Fighting pollution is just good sense and good business," Mr. Alden said.

"Then Wednesday night it is, at six o'clock," Frank said. "There are no buses passing through at that hour, so I can put my mind on my cooking. I would invite you to my little house, but the smell of the river is so bad there close to the factory, you wouldn't enjoy it. But we can have a good time at the bus station."

Benny felt as if he could hardly wait for Wednesday to come. He wondered what Frank would serve for dinner. Hamburgers? That wouldn't be a treat.

At six o'clock Henry parked the car beside the bus station door.

The wind was coming from the north, so there was no bad smell in the air.

Benny was the first one out of the car. He hardly had a chance to rap on the door when Frank opened it. He greeted all the Aldens.

"Hello, hello," he said. "Right on time."

"We've been looking forward to this all week," Benny said. "And does it smell good in here!"

"It's the fish," Frank replied with a smile. "I bought it at the best market in town. I stuffed it with soft breadcrumbs mixed with butter and salt and spice—"

"And everything nice," Violet finished.

"Yes, and now it is baking. In a few minutes it will be done to a turn."

The Aldens saw that Frank had set his biggest table for six. There were real plates and a tablecloth. No paper plates or cups tonight.

Grandfather looked around and smiled.

"Sit right down," said Frank, going into his kitchen.

Everyone took a seat, and soon Frank began to bring platters of food to his guests.

"Everything came from my own garden," Frank said, putting a plate of baked potatoes on the table. Next came a large dish filled with all kinds of vegetables.

Benny began to count them up. "Carrots, little onions, beets, parsley. And look! Cowslips!"

"I canned the cowslips last year," Frank said proudly. "They came from the riverbank on the other side of the factory. But you can't see dessert yet. It's in the refrigerator. It's a mystery dessert."

"A mystery dessert sounds like fun," said Violet.

"I bet it's ice cream," said Benny.

"I bet it isn't," said Frank.

This was a new Frank. He was happy and joking. Now he knew Mr. Pickett was going to stop pouring dirty water into the river. He knew that many people wanted to save the river and understood how important it was. He could sit back and enjoy the first company dinner he ever served.

"Vinegar," Benny said. "For my cowslips. And lemon juice, too."

"Lemon is for the fish," Frank said. He put the baked fish on the table. After serving the fish with an old-fashioned pie knife, Frank sat down.

Henry and Frank and Mr. Alden talked together. But Benny kept wondering what the mystery dessert could be. He had guessed who Jud's and Troy's father was, but he couldn't guess what the dessert was. It was in the refrigerator, but it wasn't ice cream. And Frank wouldn't tell what it was.

Benny thought, "I'm sure it isn't a pudding, and I don't think it could be a pie or a cake. I guess I'll just have to wait." That was hard to do. But he enjoyed every bit of Frank's fish and stuffing.

All the Aldens enjoyed the delicious dinner Frank had cooked. Soon their plates were clean.

"Let me help you clear off the table," said Jessie.

"I'll clear," said Frank, "and you can pile the dishes up. You'll see where they go in that sink."

Then the moment came when Frank opened the refrigerator to get dessert. Benny twisted around in his seat to see what it was.

"A watermelon!" he exclaimed. "But you never raised that, Frank."

"Oh, yes, I did!" laughed Frank. "You can go down to my garden and pick one any time now. I'm going to sell some of them."

"We'll buy one, for sure," Violet said. "We just love watermelon."

Everyone took a slice of watermelon, and soon it was gone, except for the green rind. "I save that," said Frank. "I make watermelon pickle out of it."

"What about that!" said Benny. He snapped a watermelon seed across the room.

"I wouldn't do that, Ben," said Mr. Alden in a low voice. "This is really Frank's bus station, and he'll have to sweep it up."

"I don't mind," said Frank, snapping a seed in Benny's direction.

Soon even Grandfather was snapping watermelon seeds!

"What a party," thought Jessie. "I don't know when I have seen Grandfather having such a good time."

When everyone was tired of snapping seeds, Frank swept them up. Jessie and Violet said they would wash the dishes. But Frank had a dishwasher, so the work was soon done.

"We ought to have a fish party next year," said Benny. "Maybe at our house."

"Maybe at *my* house," said Frank. "By next year it will be lovely down there by the river. We might even catch our own fish."

"Hooray!" said Benny. "Grandfather and I love to go fishing. Let's make it a real date. What about my birthday? That's the fifteenth of July."

"I'll write it right down in my book," said Mr.

Alden, taking out his wallet. In a small notebook he wrote, "July 15. Fishing with Benny and Frank."

"I can remember that," said Frank. "I don't need to write it down."

A little later the Aldens said good-bye to Frank and drove home in their station wagon.

"Everything turned out right," said Benny. "Don't you think so, Grandfather?"

"Yes, Ben, it did," Mr. Alden answered. "I think the river will be saved. And I think Mr. Pickett will be able to make the changes in his factory. He'll be Frank's good neighbor after all."

"I never guessed those two boys were Picketts," said Jessie. "Frank didn't trust the boys because he thought they were on their father's side. But really, they picketed their own father's business."

"Pickett's pickets," said Benny with a laugh. "You know, most of this adventure was just an accident. We would never have known Frank or the Pickett family or learned about the paint factory or started to clean up the river . . ."

"If the bus hadn't been late," finished Henry.

"Right," said Benny.

About the Author

GERTRUDE CHANDLER WARNER discovered when she was teaching that many readers who like an exciting story could find no books that were both easy and fun to read. She decided to try to meet this need, and her first book, *The Boxcar Children*, quickly proved she had succeeded.

Miss Warner drew on her own experiences to write the mystery. As a child she spent hours watching trains go by on the tracks opposite her family home. She often dreamed about what it would be like to set up housekeeping in a caboose or freight car—the situation the Alden children find themselves in.

When Miss Warner received requests for more adventures involving Henry, Jessie, Violet, and Benny Alden, she began additional stories. In each, she chose a special setting and introduced unusual or eccentric characters who liked the unpredictable.

While the mystery element is central to each of Miss Warner's books, she never thought of them as strictly juvenile mysteries. She liked to stress the Aldens' independence and resourcefulness and their solid New England devotion to using up and making do. The Aldens go about most of their adventures with as little adult supervision as possible—something else that delights young readers.

Miss Warner lived in Putnam, Connecticut, until her death in 1979. During her lifetime, she received hundreds of letters from girls and boys telling her how much they liked her book. And so she continued the Aldens' adventures, writing a total of nineteen books in the Boxcar Children series.